HARRY
the Dirty Dog

HARRY

by Gene Zion

the Dirty Dog

Pictures by Margaret Bloy Graham

HarperCollins*Publishers*

HARRY THE DIRTY DOG
Text copyright © 1956 by Eugene Zion,
renewed 1984 by Ruth Zion Frischer
Illustrations copyright © 1956, 1984 by Margaret Bloy Graham
Recolorization copyright © 2002 by Margaret Bloy Graham
Printed in the United States of America. All rights reserved.
For information address HarperCollins Children's Books,
a division of HarperCollins Publishers,
195 Broadway, New York, NY 10007.
www.harperchildrens.com
Library of Congress catalog card number: 56-8137
ISBN 0-06-026865-4
ISBN 0-06-026866-2 (lib. bdg.)
ISBN 0-06-443009-X (pbk.)
❖

14 15 16 17 18 LP/WOR 50 49 48 47 46 45 44 43 42 41

Harry was a white dog with black spots
who liked everything,
except . . . getting a bath.
So one day when he heard the water
running in the tub,
he took the scrubbing brush . . .

and buried it in the backyard.

Then he ran away from home.

He played where they were fixing the street

and got very dirty.

He played at the railroad

and got even dirtier.

He played tag with other dogs

and became dirtier still.

He slid down a coal chute
and got the dirtiest of all.
In fact, he changed

from a white dog with black spots
to a black dog with white spots.

Although there were many other things to do,
Harry began to wonder if his family thought
that he had *really* run away.

He felt tired and hungry too,
so without stopping on the way
he ran back home.

When Harry got to his house,
he crawled through the fence
and sat looking at the back door.

One of the family looked out and said,
"There's a strange dog in the backyard . . .
by the way, has anyone seen Harry?"

When Harry heard this, he tried very hard
to show them *he* was Harry. He started to do
all his old, clever tricks. He flip-flopped

and he flop-flipped.
He rolled over and played dead.

He danced and he sang.

He did these tricks over and over again,
but everyone shook their heads and said,
"Oh no, it couldn't be Harry."

Harry gave up
and walked slowly toward the gate,
but suddenly he stopped.

He ran to a corner of the garden
and started to dig furiously.
Soon he jumped away from the hole
barking short, happy barks.

He'd found the scrubbing brush!
And carrying it in his mouth,
he ran into the house.

Up the stairs he dashed,
with the family
following close behind.

He jumped into the bathtub and sat up begging,
with the scrubbing brush in his mouth,
a trick he certainly had never done before.

"This little doggie wants a bath!"
cried the little girl, and her father said,
"Why don't you and your brother give him one?"

Harry's bath was the soapiest one he'd ever had.
It worked like magic. As soon as the children
started to scrub, they began shouting,
"Mummy! Daddy! Look, look! Come quick!"

"It's Harry! It's Harry! It's Harry!" they cried.
Harry wagged his tail and was very, very happy.
His family combed and brushed him lovingly, and
he became once again a white dog with black spots.

It was wonderful to be home.
After dinner, Harry fell asleep
in his favorite place, happily dreaming
of how much fun it had been getting dirty.
He slept so soundly,
he didn't even feel the scrubbing brush
he'd hidden under his pillow.